FARNHAM FLASH FESTIVAL 2022

Longlist

Introduction

The Farnham Flash Fiction competition is an exciting and highly competitive literary event that is a part of the Farnham Fringe Festival. The competition challenges writers to create compelling and engaging works of fiction, all within the constraints of just 500 words.

Open to writers from all around the world, the Farnham Flash Fiction competition attracts some of the best new talent in the field of fiction. From emerging writers to seasoned veterans, the competition offers a platform for writers to showcase their creativity, imagination, and storytelling prowess.

With a six-month submission window running from January to June, the competition offers plenty of time for writers to craft and perfect their entries. Once the submission period ends, a team of judges sifts through the entries to find the very best, with the top 25 entries being included in a published collection of flash fiction.

The Farnham Flash Fiction competition is a must-enter event for anyone who loves writing and wants to see their work published and celebrated. Whether you're a seasoned writer or just starting out, this competition offers a unique opportunity to challenge yourself, hone your skills, and showcase your talent to a global audience. So why not enter today and see where your writing could take you?

Search: Farnham Flash Fiction competition

Contents

FARNHAM FLASH FESTIVAL 2022 3
Longlist 3
Introduction 5
A Virtuoso Performance by Ian Joynes 9
And the Winner is… by Maria Dean 11
Charms For Guarding Against Sprites by Andrew Deathe 13
Don't Pay the Ferryman by David Rowlandson 15
Driving Instruction by Daphne Larner 17
Eggs Over Sleazy by Kevin Cheeseman 19
Falling for a Pink-haired Angel by David Higham 21
Family Tree by Rob Nisbet 23
Goldie and the Inappropriate Behaviour by Margaret Goddard ... 25
Good Night Irina by Morgan Brennan 27
Gunner by Julie Evans 29
How to be like other people by Josie Lane 31
Just Not Cricket by John Glander 33
Made it to the seaside by Patrick Larsimont 35
Midnight Party by Anita Goodfellow 37
Mr Antonio's Day At The Races by Tamsin Sinclair 39
My Hair by Chrissy Sturt 41
Rachel's Visit by Marjorie Clifford 43
The House That Saved a Life by Lindsay Bertram 45
The Nearly Mother and her Woolly Jumpers by Denise Telford . 47
The Night Marie Flew by Dee Holmes 49
The Wonder of Woolies by Fay Dickinson 51
What's In A Name by John Bunting 53
While I Wait at the Bus Stop by Lorraine Collins 55

Black Matilda by Patrick Larismont 57
Farnham is Full by Anne Banks 59
Missing by Dr Sarah Law 61
The Anniversary by Richard Fuller 63
The East Street Lamp's monologue by David Rowlandson 65

2022

Overall Winner

Julie Evans : Gunner

Runner-Up

Chris Cottom : How to make a Dad Quilt

Winner - Farnham Competition

Richard Fuller : The Anniversary

Shortlist

Chris Cottom: How to make a Dad Quilt

Andrew Deathe: Charms for guarding against Sprites

Anita Goodfellow: Midnight Party

Chrissy Sturt: My Hair

Denise Telford: The Nearly Mothers and the Woolly Jumpers

Josie Lane: How To Be Like Other People

Lorraine Collins: While I Wait at the Bus Stop

Margaret Goddard: Goldie and the Inapproriate Behavior

Rob Nisbet: Family Tree

Julie Evans: Gunner

A Virtuoso Performance by Ian Joynes

As the fairy lights around them suddenly dimmed, Rosa calmly gazed up at the night sky and sighed. An infinite number of stars twinkled back at her from the heavens. Her heart had never felt like this before. Despite the cool breeze, it was strangely beautiful out here tonight. Even the moon somehow seemed bigger, brighter and more romantic as they listened to the quintet of musicians, playing tempestuously to them like they'd never played before.

Hand in hand, Rosa and Charles sat alone at their table, toasting the ensemble of violinists and cellists assembled before them, ready to begin their final piece. The seats around them were empty now. Everyone else had chosen to leave, but Rosa and Charles were staying until the very end. How she wished the moment could last forever. If only time could stand still, for they were in love, and nothing else mattered.

It was well past midnight, as Rosa gathered her shawl tightly around her shoulders and looked devotedly across at Charles, so handsome in his elegant dinner suit. He looked cold too, but there wasn't long to go now.

'I'll never forget this moment' Rosa whispered, gently squeezing his hand. 'I shall always remember it, until my dying day.'

Charles smiled lovingly back, but said nothing, his distant mind somewhere else, deep in thought.

Time between them was so precious. Being here together, alone for as long as they could was what they both wanted. It felt dignified, the honourable thing to do, and they had no desire to disrespect the band, for without an audience they no longer had a purpose.

It was the band's fine virtuoso performance that had kept them both so strong. For there was no point on lamenting on things that couldn't be changed. Just let the music play and others worry about their pointless hectic lives.

Rosa knew the final piece, 'Nearer My God to Thee.' It was a hymn, but one she recognised more as a requiem, its haunting theme helping mask some of the creaking and groaning sounds coming from the great ship beneath them, starting its final descent below the waves.

The decks of the Titanic were gradually slipping lower and lower into the sea, and the seats upon which they were sitting, gently being washed away, one by one.

As the water lapped at their feet, Rosa and Charles braced themselves for whatever the future had in store.

'I love you' Charles declared. 'I just want you to know.'

'I do' Rosa smiled. 'And I love you too.'

But their performance was finally over, the music had stopped. It was time for them to go now, just like everyone else. Time only for one last embrace between them, one final kiss goodbye.

For the great ship was disappearing, on its way down to its final resting place on the bottom, leaving behind just the screams and memories of its passengers struggling in the icy waters above.

And the Winner is… by Maria Dean

"I take it that we have no more suggestions?" Roger projected his voice far enough across the table that it jolted Mabel awake, her neck creaking as she sat bolt upright. He was met with an aging silence that seemed to have taken up residence long before the meeting had begun. "It's decided then." Roger jabbed the end of his pencil on the table as if it were a gavel.

"What's decided?" Derek asked pushing his glasses back up his nose for the hundredth time that morning.

Roger stared at Derek and let out an audible sigh making a noise much like a slowly deflating airbed. "We have decided that the only way to tackle the saboteur is if we all take it in turns to patrol the allotment every night until the day of the competition." Roger waited a few seconds before he added, "It was *your* idea, Derek."

"And a good one too," Sue chipped in, her rheumy eyes roaming the room considering where to land. "I'm in with a good chance of winning this year; my marrow is a beauty. I shall have to get Roy to bring it in in the wheelbarrow on competition day."

"I'll wager that it is not as big as mine!" Fred croaked from the far corner, a mischievous grin spreading across his face, contorting his lined wrinkles into deep trenches.

"I will draw up a rota," Roger interrupted as he surveyed the rest of his rivals. "And mark my words," he proclaimed with pompous gusto, "if any weed-killing wielding vandals try to sabotage the Farnham vegetable competition this year, then we will catch them red-handed!" His speech was met with the clatter of Joan's knitting needles falling on the floor and the crackle of a Werther's Original wrapper.

"Meeting adjourned," Roger announced, his eyes narrowing behind his varifocal lenses.

He looked on at the septuagenarian patrol unit. Veronica was digging around in her handbag, looking for a pair of glasses that were pushed messily on top of her head, Sue's hearing aid whistled an annoying monotone hum whilst she returned to this morning's Sudoku and Dave shuffled off to the toilet, his prostate giving him gyp again.

They weren't exactly the Home Guard.

Roger grinned, safe in the knowledge that he would retain his title, just as long as he didn't run out of weed killer.

Charms For Guarding Against Sprites by Andrew Deathe

Crosby wanted to stop the fairies from coming into his cottage and causing mischief. He paid great attention to the lore that kept them away. He never whistled indoors. He never brought sprays of mayflower into the house. But still he worried that the little people would get in.

Beside the path outside his home, Crosby planted a bush of grey sage. The herb's scent was known to be obnoxious to the pucks. It was claimed that they couldn't bear to be near it, in case it brushed against them and tainted their skin and clothes, so that even their own kind would avoid them. The creatures thought that this was nonsense, however. They would come to the shrub each evening and pick the pungent leaves to rub under their arms, to keep the flies away. The plant never thrived.

Crosby tied a red thread to a post of the porch outside his door. This was alleged to prevent those who crossed the border with the otherworld from crossing his threshold. In fact, the elvenkind loved the colour red. They gnawed and worried the cotton until it broke loose, then braided it through their hair or stitched it into their clothes. Crosby always replaced the cord when it went missing. This happened often, because the fay grew ever fonder of it.

Crosby left a single boot on his doorstep. Putting on just one shoe supposedly confused the grey folk, causing them to walk in circles. The fair tribe scoffed at this idea and used the boot as a lavatory. Their urine smelt of autumn rain and floated with bits of brown leaf. Crosby emptied the boot several times and kept it on the step. Eventually a pixie kicked it under the scrubby sage bush, where it lay, uselessly, for months.

Along the cottage windowsills, Crosby drew thick lines with a beeswax candle. He knew that the darklings could not cross this magical barrier. But the citizens of Faerie had not been informed of this fable. Indeed, they were attracted to the warm, honeyed smell of the wax. They scraped it up with their long fingernails and rolled it into small balls. They sniffed it, and squidged it, and flicked it at each other for sport as they unlatched the windows to let their compatriots into the house.

Hanging by the fire, Crosby kept a shallow iron pan, in which he cooked his breakfast every morning. He was told by the old people in the village that the devil and his witches, and all the hobs and changelings that associated with them, hated and feared iron. To touch it would dissolve them and they would shrink away at the sight of it. Crosby thought nothing of that tale; superstition and nonsense it was. But the heavy pan did make the perfect swat when it came to battering the little bastards, which he could so easily do when they were too busy playing with wax balls to notice him waiting for them.

Don't Pay the Ferryman by David Rowlandson

Don't pay the Ferryman. At least not until you get to the other side. The words went around and around inside the head of the sole passenger on the ferryboat. The chain ferry had carried passengers across the dangerous river for many a year. On one side sat civilisation. On the other? Most local persons would never set foot there. Most didn't.

"What's a young man like you doing crossing here?" enquired the weather beaten, grey-haired old ferryman as his gloved hands heaved on the cable.

Rubbing his cold hands together the redheaded traveller solemnly answered, without looking up. "Not much else left for me to do. Just got out of prison, see. No-one wants me around. It's not as if I could start a new life. Is it? Anywhere is better than being here."

Don't pay the Ferryman. Not yet. The redhead only had the money charitably given to him on release. A shilling fare would make a big dent in his purse.

Without looking at his passenger, the ferryman remarked, "It's dangerous, they say. On the other side I mean." The redhead didn't care.

"And? It's not as if my life is worth anything is it?" The ex-convict returned to his self-pitying thoughts. *A shilling. That's a big dent in my meagre monies.*

Don't pay.

Subconsciously he fiddled with his purse, spilling what monies he had on the slippery wet deck of the ferryboat. The ferryman never said a word. Just watched, and pulled on the cable, as the redhead swore and gathered up the coins. The diminishing light of the late evening disappeared and the traveller's journey moved into dark shadows.

As the ferryboat approached the riverbank, the ferryman remarked, in what the redhead felt was so like the menacing manner of the cruel warders, much witnessed during his incarceration. "At least you have the coinage to pay me. A shilling! Unless you want to give me more. I won't object."

Don't.

The young man's nightmares were being acted out. He had been warned that some passengers ferried to the other side were never seen again. *Is this it? My final moments.* He stood up, as straight as he could muster, waiting for the blow that would give him the peace he craved.

Nobody heard the splash of the body entering the river's fast flowing waters. At that moment there were no other passengers, no witnesses. The new, young, gloved, redheaded Ferryman breathed a sigh of relief. "Who said you can't start a new life?"

Driving Instruction by Daphne Larner

It was just a game of 'Pretend' to the children after they noticed a key still in the ignition of Grandpa's car in the driveway. They had peered in through the windows, opened the doors, and two of them sat inside, winding down the glass using the chrome handles. There was a whiff of old leather within which added to reminiscence of journeys they had been on, with Grandpa driving.

All the adults were inside the bungalow, musing over his funeral. There were quiet suggestions being made as to how newly widowed Grandma might best be cared for in the future.

'Do they think I'm deaf, as well as senile?' she asked herself. She sidled out of the front door with an urgent desire to escape, attracted by the sound of young voices outside.

Seeking sanctuary, she plonked herself into the driver's seat, invigorated by the children's welcoming babble. They felt a shared sadness at Grandpa's sudden passing. They should cheer her up…. she deserved it.

Suddenly everyone under 10 was on board the capacious estate car. They goaded her to start it up, so she released the handbrake to roll forwards. The car crunched over the gravel drive towards the open gates. As the engine growled into action there was a rash of mourners at her bungalow's bay windows, peering out. Their alarmed response had been slowed by the free alcohol flowing from Grandpa's well stocked bar in the lounge. They stared frozen, in abject disbelief, as the car turned sharply right on to the road outside.

It was too late by the time sprightly Uncle Geoffrey had pushed his way through the throng in the hallway. From the front door he made a dash down the driveway.

The vintage car he had secretly craved ownership of for many years had disappeared. He had driven it round the local lanes this morning to check its performance. Now he could only think about its potentially perilous journey packed with the families' progeny. His hands trembled as he punched down digits for the emergency services on his mobile.

Grandma had only meant to clock up a few miles, but the sign said 'Smart motorway', so she assumed it meant a safer road.

'Put your foot down!' they yelled with enthusiasm from the back seats.

'Put your seat belts on' she cautioned, reminded that health and safety might be a significant factor in this adventure, like trying to eat steak without your teeth in. She had no idea why she thought of this analogy.

'Pomp the gas' cried the five-year-old, wriggling with excitement on her sister's lap.

'I've got no licence!' confessed Grandma, shouting: 'I lost it at 73'

'Don't worry Grandma, I'm sure it's in a drawer somewhere in your house.'

'We can't see any cops…'

'We'll fly like Batman and Robin!'

'Look at those cars flashing us' they cried and waved back at them.

Such nonsense they talk, she thought with a sigh, overtaking a Porsche.

Eggs Over Sleazy by Kevin Cheeseman

Primed with a fresh hit of cocaine, Jake's heart was beating faster than the pounding dance music. He shoved through the crowd to where he'd last seen Dean.

Jake had left his mate chatting up a blonde in an eye-catching, zebra print jumpsuit. She may have had a couple of years on them, but she was a stunner and no mistake.

'Out of your league, Dean,' he'd said. But he'd been wrong apparently – they were nowhere to be seen. Well, if Dean could get lucky, so could he.

Jake prowled around the edge of the dance floor and soon spotted two likely-looking girls. He moved in, wondering which one would fall for his well-honed banter. He'd been practising his lines all day.

But when they heard his slick patter, the girls looked at him in disgust.

'Are you friggin' serious?'

'You can't say that sort of thing these days, sunshine. Sod off.'

Jake swore at them and beat a retreat to the bar.

Two shots later, he was back in the fray. And there she was again: the blonde in the jumpsuit. No sign of Dean. She must have blown him out, after all.

'Make way for the master,' he murmured.

He slid over and put his hand on the small of her back. She turned and looked at him expectantly.

'Hey, sweet cheeks,' said Jake, 'how do you like your eggs in the morning? Because I'll be making you breakfast.'

After a pitch-perfect delivery, he was dismayed when she signalled that she hadn't heard what he'd said.

'Sorry,' she said, 'it's a bit loud in here.'

Jake leaned in close. Her perfume was heady. He took a breath and repeated his favourite line.

She smiled. 'That's what I thought you said.'

Result.

Jake barely had time to spot her nod at someone behind him before unseen hands gripped his arms. He was forced through the crowd and out to the pavement. He gasped as the cold night air hit him. He gasped again as the blonde produced a warrant card from her jumpsuit.

'Detective Sergeant Ross. You're under arrest for offences under the Sexual Harassment Act 2025. Put him in the van, boys. I'll meet you at the station.'

When the van doors were opened, Jake saw Dean, hands cuffed behind his back, staring out at him.

'The blonde bit?' asked Dean.

Jake nodded.

At the police station, the custody sergeant told Jake he'd be spending the night in the cells. His cocaine high fast fading, Jake felt dazed and despondent, and he was grateful that the constable who took him to his cell treated him so gently. The old copper asked Jake for his belt and shoelaces and brought him a cup of tea. Advising Jake to get some sleep, he exited the cell and locked the door. Then he slid the observation hatch open.

'Sorry, Jake, I forgot to ask,' – his face broke into a grin – 'how do you like your eggs in the morning?'

Falling for a Pink-haired Angel by David Higham

When George had been sitting at the top of the stairs, car towrope in shaking, clammy hand, the last thing he had expected to discover was that angels wore dark green paramedic uniforms and had pink hair. But there she was staring down at him out of the light and, oddly for an angel, trying to break his ribs by pumping his chest really hard. It hurt.

'Can you tell me your name?' She asked.

It took a while for him to work out whose name she wanted. Then, despite the raging pain in his neck, he tried to say George but only an agonising croak came through his wrecked larynx.

Can't even do myself in right, George thought.

The bright sunlight streaming through the curtains faded and he slipped back towards the dark. Images flashed before him. He saw the note his wife had left for him on the kitchen table, '...*can't take any more ... need space. I need some excitement in my life. I'm leaving ....*' George knew he had been no better as a husband than as a salesman. On target earnings? If he had ever made target he might have been able to satisfy her expensive tastes. Needless to say, he never had.

He had never made her happy in the bedroom either and hadn't she made that obvious? He saw his worthless son slamming the front door as he left. Rubbish father he may have been but she had always spoiled the boy. He saw himself alone in the house dragging his feet upstairs for what he intended to be the last time.

The images dissolved and the black returned. He was falling into an abyss. Then he thought he heard a faint voice calling from far above him,

'George, George, stay with me!'

Staring up, he saw a faint pinprick of white light and the voice seemed to be coming from up there. He remembered the angel and the kind grey eyes beneath the pink fringe. He decided that he had something to live for, gripped the sides of the tunnel and started to climb fingertip by fingertip up towards the light. The pain was awful. His arms ached and his fingers were raw. A great weight was dragging him down towards the dark but still he pulled and pulled.

It took an age, but George eventually reached the light.

'He's back.' He heard the voice clearly now. He opened his eyes.
"Thought we'd lost you, pet,' said the pink-haired angel and George knew that, perhaps for the first time, he was in love.

Family Tree by Rob Nisbet

Dad says he planted the apple tree the day I was born, grown from a pip. There was a comparison every birthday to see which of us was taller: the tree won every time. Last year I tried to climb it, but I fell and gashed a scar down my left arm. Not the tree's fault; I should have been more careful.

Dad says the tree and I are twins, but with different lifespans, it could outlive me several times. We are both twelve now. The tree may be bigger, but Dad says it's still a child. It is still way taller than me; Dad says I will grow more this year than any other. He's right, I can easily reach that first branch, but I'm not sure that's what he meant. There is another fork in the trunk higher up, and that's where I sit looking out over the fence.

A man walks past, young I guess, with a woman on his arm. She waddles, pregnant and bulging. They see me watching behind the clusters of white blossom. "I climbed trees at your age." He wears a t-shirt and I can see that *his* left arm is scarred too. "I used to have a shelf in my tree," he adds, "for a snack."

I tell Dad and he fits an old tray in place, suspended on garden string. I visit the tree every day and take up a sandwich for my lunch. I watch the flowers bulge into baby apples, round like that waddling woman. People wander below me, and I wonder if *I'll* ever walk past, with a girl on my arm.

The apples ripen to a burning red over the summer. I don't bring sandwiches up here anymore. I've outgrown that. But I still like to look out beyond the fence, the world is so much larger than my little garden. There is an old man who walks by with a dog. They are both slow. I decide to get a dog, too, when I'm as old as him. I'll call it Benji. The dog barks up, and I am spotted among the crispy autumn leaves. "Throw me an apple," calls the old man. "I want it for the pips." I pick the biggest, reddest apple. He catches it awkwardly in his left hand; I guess that his arm might be scarred too. "I want to leave a tree, growing in my garden," he says. "Something that will outlive me."

"Have you had a good life?" I ask. It seems important somehow.

He nods and smiles. He gives me a wave then walks off with the dog. "Come on, Ben," he says.

I don't know whether he plants the pips or not. Even in the winter, I sometimes climb the bare branches, looking out at the world beyond the fence, but I don't see him again.

Goldie and the Inappropriate Behaviour by Margaret Goddard

Goldie picked her way down the dark forest path.

She was barefoot. The silver Manolo knock-offs had been a disaster and her feet had rebelled. The others had giddily forged ahead without her and she'd been forced into abandoning her shoes. She'd walked on careful tiptoe along damply stained pavements in a vain attempt to keep up.

She'd shouted,

"Hey wait! Wait for me!" as her so-called friends crowded into a couple of cabs and sped away. She didn't have enough money for a taxi of her own and her phone was dead. She'd stood and cursed at length; then after considering all available options she'd turned onto the woodland path that led home.

Stopping to disentangle her waist-length hair extensions from a disrespectful branch, she spotted a building amid the trees. Dry-throated from a hovering hangover, she pushed on the door of the lone cottage shouting, *he-llo?*

She had a long drink of water straight from the tap. There was nobody home, but here were three odd sized chairs around a table with three bowls of porridge in three diminishing sizes. Strange. She collapsed into the biggest chair. Oh, it was so good to rest her poor feet.

She tasted the porridge in the biggest bowl, grimaced and spat it out. Salty! She gagged on the sickly-sweet slop in the mid-sized bowl, but the porridge in the smallest bowl was delicious. Creamy, sweetened with honey

She ate the lot. She stood up too quickly. Her head swam, she tripped and fell onto the littlest chair. It broke. She banged her elbow, her feet hurt and she was feeling truly awful. She really needed to lie down.

Upstairs, there were beds in different sizes. She wrinkled her nose at the biggest bed, it reeked of sweaty feet. The middle sized bed crackled with crumbs and there was a sandwich under the pillow. The smallest, softest bed had a lavender scented pillow, she lay down, spread out her damp hair, tucked her feet under the blanket and, sighing with contentment, she fell into a deep sleep.

The Bear family returned home to find they'd had an intruder. Mrs Bear scolded her husband for not locking the door, Baby Bear sobbed for the double loss of his little chair and his bowl of porridge. Mr Bear armed himself with a stout umbrella, Mrs Bear chose her heaviest rolling pin.

The family crept upstairs.

Baby whispered,

"Look! A real mermaid! On my bed."

Goldie, clad in body-hugging silver lamé, woke, vomited a rainbow torrent of porridge, red-wine, cranberry juice and a half-digested fish kebab.

She croaked,

"Water! I must have water!"

"I knew it!" shouted Baby.

Good Night Irina by Morgan Brennan

Someday, comrades, civilization will understand my work here in Urals.

This evening, I have one duty left to perform. Yury sleeps like a babushka and won't disturb me. It's been a well-executed plan, though I say so myself. Much better than our glorious leader's special military operation into Nazi Ukraine, and all that fuss from Western media. You'd have thought we'd started a war. They don't understand the difference between a military operation and all-out war.

I will miss Irina and told her not to wait up. We were very upset. We knew life would be bad for Mother Russia when Macdonald's closed and then Coke and Starbucks and even Netflix pulled their plug. Irina loved The Crown—British comedy at its best. And the straw that broke this "Bears" back—no Eurovision. Every year we watch it with that funny man, what's-is-name, Graham Norman on BBC while consuming a "Maccy D". There is nothing left for us now—except bloody ballet.

As Major Andreyev Ivanov, 31st Rocket Army, I have huge responsibility. Missile Silo 12 is in secret location outside Orenburg. Oops, now I will have to shoot myself. I'm kidding, comrades. Irena and I have no children, so my two babies are Sarmat RS-28 ICBMs. Each missile has ten megatons of nuclear warheads. One baby is for London and the other for Los Angeles.

We were a proud country once, and now we are humiliated. Our vodka is best in world, yet we can't even export no more—so I drink.

'Nostrovia!'

I am ready, comrades. I told Yury it was a drill— "another bloody drill, Yury". So he turns his key same time as me. We input codes. Turn more keys together and the launch button lights up red and alarm sounds—I laced his vodka with a sleeping powder and it worked like a Roma's charm.

"Don't worry, Yury," I told him, "test is successful, have well-earned rest."

I stand at console. *Now I am become Death, the destroyer of worlds.*

Someone bangs on silo doors. They're reinforced Yekaterinburg steel.

'Major Ivanov, sir, open up. Moscow's on the hotline.'

It's not too late, comrades. I could open the doors with green button and launch is aborted and I am court marshalled, but I *will* see Irina again.

'Major, open now, or we'll blow the bloody doors off.'

I have a minute, maybe less. If I press red button, then it's bye bye, dear Boris, Your Majesty, Sir Andrew Murray, Dame Judi, Hugh Grant, Michael bloody-doors-off Caine; and farewell, LA Dodgers, Harry and Meghan, California Beachboys, Johnny Depp and Tom goody-shoes Hanks—your boys will take one hell of a beating.

'Major, President Putin's orders. Abort at once or we detonate.'

I press button.

Gunner by Julie Evans

Gunner is sixteen but tall enough to be old enough and keen as Colman's, as they say. He stands behind the screen, coughs, puffs out, reads the letters on the chart. 20/20 says the doctor. You're A1. Tip top. When they look for scars, moles, tattoos, he never thinks, this is how they will know me. *Crescent scar: Back of right hand* (a slip with the chisel).

At the sound of that first reveille, he wakes up amongst men who talk about women while they brush their teeth and shave their stubbly chins. He watches the muscles in their shoulders ripple in the mirror. He doesn't tell them that he's still a virgin, that he can only imagine the things they speak of.

On the training ground, when that first eighteen pounder explodes, he holds his body tight and still despite the sonic boom reverberating through every still-growing cell. Months later, from the deck of the troopship, he watches the white fringe of his homeland disappear, soothing the horses, his hands on their necks while they whinny and rear at the roll of the waves. When the ship is torpedoed, he swims away from the bodies, the burning oil, the flotsam, newt-like from his boyish summers in the reservoir, rescued to be fed back in, foddered.

On land, he digs holes: latrines, dug outs, gun pits, ammunition dumps. He swears at the blisters on his hands, at the burn on his neck from the mean Gallic sun, but the sun is no match for the rain that clogs the arteries of the land with mud so dense that billy-goats drown. It takes all six of them to drag the gun through the gloop and the farm horse cries with the effort, his legs like brittle sticks, nostrils flaring with alarm.

He writes home while smoking on his bunk, inhaling the harsh tobacco of the Woodbines handed out by the chaplain along with the New Testament. He never opens the book. In his letters, he doesn't mention the stinks: cordite, gas, mud, shit; the itch of lice; the foot rot. He writes instead of sunrise and camaraderie, asks if little Marjorie has her first tooth yet, if Jimmy has caught a rabbit for the pot.

He's two years in when a bell rings in his ear and his mouth is full of earth and everything goes slow. The bearers step uncertainly, jolting the stretcher as they duck bullets. There's a huge pain somewhere that he can't locate. A torn flap of uniform blows across his thigh, and he worries about how hard it will be to sew back.

In Gunner's war, he cries only once: when he thinks of that telegram lad, Jonny Macalister, fast-pedalling his bicycle, pink-cheeked with news; of the women gasping as he passes their front doors; of his mother turning from her washing line, dropping her pegs, clutching a pair of laundered bloomers tight to her chest.

How to be like other people by Josie Lane

Row A, Seat 16

    I sit in isolation. Back row, tucked in the far left-hand corner under the dimmed cinema lights. It's my safe space. No one can pass me. Most people don't want to be next to the solitary seat that I always book online, so there's usually plenty of elbow room. Films are my obsession.

    I watch heads emerging from the tunnel, turning like ants weaving towards their destination. Hands clutch oversized cartons of coke and boxes spewing popcorn, resembling yellow puckered lumps of lava. The smell of candy, caffeine and cheesy tangs fills the air. The opening crackle of sweet wrappers muffles soft chattering. I've always hung around the fringes, staring at the world around me but never really belonging.

    It's the same at my ASD support group for high functioning autistic teens. I'm willing to listen in a circle but don't participate much. Our therapist is cool with that. The only time I'm expected to talk is when we read out the notes. These are questions handed in anonymously by members into the 'Curious' box at the beginning of each session. It's mostly boring social stuff about regular people and how to fit in with them. So dull. But that all changed when Izzy joined three months ago.

    I was dazzled by the waves of her shiny, honey-coloured hair and electric blue eyes. She buzzed like a bee and her conversations swerved off at tangents like a volleyball before bouncing back to the group discussion. Her delicate hands fluttered as she spoke. After revealing her addiction to films, my seventeen-year-old self was blown away. She swirled around in my everyday thoughts, clouding my perspective. For the first time in my life, I considered connecting.

    I spent hours rehearsing friendly chat-up lines from movies in my bedroom mirror but froze in Izzy's presence whenever there was a chance to talk. I caught her eye once and forced an unnatural grin mimicking one of my favourite actors, but she appeared to look through me and carried on talking to the others. I blushed cherry red, feeling crushed. She probably thought I was weird. Everyone else does. I bolted for the exit after the meeting ended when someone called out my name.

    "Hey, Carlo." The voice was unmistakable.

I turned around, quaking.

Izzy smiled. "I hear you're really into films."

"Yeah…a bit like you."

She handed me a 'Curious' box note. "Take this. Don't read it until you get home."

I nodded and freeze-framed that scene over and over in my mind for the next week.

Row A, Seat 15

Izzy flips down the seat next to me, breathless. "Sorry. Missed the bus."

Excitement and relief fill me, and I peel a natural smile. I had booked two tickets after reading Izzy's note: *Will you go to the cinema with me?*

We've been texting ever since, sharing thoughts and dreams, and making links in our little universe. A place without constraints or conventions where we can simply just be.

Just Not Cricket by John Glander

"Howzat!"

The delivery had been fast and the ball had reared up, striking the batter on the upper arm and then the side of the head. On spinning around in a vain attempt to avoid contact with the potent missile, the bat had first demolished the stumps and then hit the wicket keeper for six.

"No ball!" the umpire intoned.

"Oh come on!" The bowler was annoyed. "The ball landed plumb in line with middle stump. Bouncing off the batter only gave them a gentle blow."

Since the batter was lying on the ground, not moving, the fact could have been disputed.

"Off balance, fell over."

The wicket keeper was trying to stem the blood pouring from the nose.

"Gentle blow!" The non-striker seemed incensed. "This is a gentle blow."

The bat whirled, catching the bowler full across the chest.

"Now there was a gentle blow."

The bowler was rolling about on the ground, screaming. The outfielders were moving in. From the pavilion, two figures holding their bats aloft, emerged at a run. At this point, probably wisely, the umpires fled the field to take shelter behind the sight screen. More of the batting team were emerging. A stump was pulled viciously from the ground and hurled, javelin like, at the rapidly approaching silly point.

A voice in the crowd yelled, "Someone call the police!"

One of the fielders screamed back, "I am the bloody police."

"Need medical help!"

There should have been some on hand, but the Saint John's Ambulance people who had been on duty seemed to have vanished. Possibly they felt the field of battle to be too dangerous. They had reason on their side. One of the spectators attempting to apply mediation, had to retire, limping and holding a delicate part. The quiet area of suburbia was erupting with yells and screams.

The score board was flashing the message, GAME ABANDONED - DRAW.

Then, above the noise resonating from the pavilion, could be heard the sounds of sirens. Black figures stormed onto the field of play. The full body armour, helmets, shields and batons were probably over kill but clearly they had been told there was a riot taking place. All out war would have been a better description. They were too late anyway, with those left standing clearly dazed, in shock and bleeding. Getting it out of the whites was going to be a major problem no matter what the smart television advertisements claimed.

Paramedics followed with stretchers and then paused, to look at the scene in amazement. Some semblance of order had been established with the police escorting people from the ground and pulling apart some who were still in dispute. The paramedics were able to move in, though prying bats out of hands proved challenging in some cases.

"Meant to be a game for gentlemen," one umpire said to his companion. "Should never allowed women to play."

His expression as she felled him with a single blow, was something to behold.

Made it to the seaside by Patrick Larsimont

What are you doing here, Dad? Mum's going to kill you for using the beach towel to carry me. I'm never allowed near the towels, especially the white ones. Feels nice though and I am a little cold. I like it when you carry me.

This is a nice spot, amongst the ivy, wildflowers and damp earth. Somewhere to dig and sniff out the red tails and tree rats. The sky is cloudless and so blue, but I don't like those screaming white birds. This bush with the pink flowers is nice and it's cool and shady, somewhere I can rest a while and maybe catch my breath.

It was tough last night. Sitting with you having a cuddle. I felt safe, but I just couldn't get enough air. I know I was annoying, but I was a scared every time things went black. It was always reassuring though to wake to someone saying, 'You OK, old Toff?' Whether it was Mum, or Lili or Lolo, or even my favourite, Nan, it's always nice to know someone cares. Even if it's just dopey brother Ted, who never makes much of a fuss, or our little Sis, who does, always trying her best to tidy me up when I've been out for a while.

I remember when me and Ted were young and living in the big city. I'd come to visit, and we'd run around the grass patch, chasing off the red ones and the whistling black birds. Ted really hated those birds. I never knew why, but he's my brother, so that was good enough for me. That's when I lived with my other family, my first Ma and Pa, and their little babies. I was happy, but then one day I came to you. Brother Ted was there, old and stinky, but still my Ted. He had a sister now, our Sis, who became a mother to us two fools.

Our job at the big house was to patrol the fence, keeping the red ones out and watching for the big killer birds who came after the fish in your pond. Sissy was the best at spotting them, but me and Ted backed her up, making a lot of noise.

I loved that house in the woods, but this one's nice too. The new green patch is by the woods where those old men hit balls with sticks. Not far away are the sands by the crashing water. There are lots of those screaming white birds there, but also children and others to play with. Always great fun, but sometimes a bit too much for old Ted and me. We get out of puff and need a little rest.

I'm a bit tired now too, Dad. Let me just lie here for a little bit and I'll come for a walk once I've had a rest. I'm glad I made it to the seaside.

RIP my old Toffee, you're a good boy.

Midnight Party by Anita Goodfellow

Sharon passes me the cider bottle. I take a couple of gulps, despite the bile rising in my throat. The beach is empty, apart from our group. School's finished and the promise of summer stretches before us. Sharon takes the bottle and tips it back. Even in the dark her blonde hair shimmers. She wriggles her bottom trying to get comfortable. She's never still. The boys look on and she laps up their attention. She's my best friend, just back from Lisbon, a school trip my parents couldn't afford. She twists the beads on her leather necklace – back and forth. She sighs.

The stones shift and Darren moves closer. He passes me his cigarette and I take a long drag. I flick my hair over my right shoulder, like Sharon does. I'm giddy.

The moon disappears and we're plunged into darkness. Darren's hand is on my leg. It moves higher. I shiver as I'm lost in a haze of Lynx body spray.

'I'm bored,' Sharon says. She puts down the empty cider bottle. 'I'm going for a swim.'

Darren's hand leaves my leg.

The moon is back out in time to show her slipping off her T-shirt. She drops it on the stones as she strides down the beach. All eyes are on her as she pauses, the water teasing her toes. She unhooks her bra and tosses it in the air. She beckons to us before plunging into the darkness with a shriek. The boys follow with a whoop. At the water's edge they stand one legged as they tug at their jeans. And then they're running, splashing through the water a mass of white flesh against the inky black.

I stand, sway and almost topple over. The stones are jagged sharp as I walk towards Sharon's laughter. I can't make out where the land ends and the sea begins. I stop when I hear the waves clawing at the shingle.

'Come on,' Sharon calls. She knows I won't, that I can't swim. But I draw closer. Darren ducks below the water and Sharon squeals as he grabs her.

In that moment I hate her.

The cold makes me catch my breath. Their voices are drowned out as the wave hits me. I lose my balance. The sea swirls and drags me down. I grasp at the stones – at anything. And then I'm on my feet and running up the beach my lungs burning. When I turn around to face the sea Sharon's gone. They're gone. I wonder at the power of my hate. I stand a moment too long before racing along the promenade and down the avenue where I hammer on the nearest front door.

Later, wrapped in blankets, Sharon and I don't look at each other as we clutch our mugs of sweet tea. We don't look at Darren's parents as the policeman takes them to another room. But we hear his mother's screams.

Mr Antonio's Day At The Races by Tamsin Sinclair

A last-minute entry into the all-comers race that year caused a flurry at the bookies: Black Magic, ridden by Mano Steele. Black Magic was bigger than the rest, so some spectators immediately picked him as the winner, while others thought his bulk would count against him on the flat.

Black Magic snorted and pawed the ground, dancing sideways. His coat and hooves shone like oil in the sun.

The stall doors flew open, releasing a blur of silks on top and galloping legs below. The experienced contenders, familiar with the track, soon pulled away. Black Magic started late, but within minutes he gained speed and closed on the frontrunners. His tail, plaited neatly before, streamed banner-like behind.

The crowd roared him on, feeling the astonishing heft of the horse as his thumping hooves vibrated the ground beneath their feet. Black Magic drew parallel with, then overtook, the leader. He won the race to cheers of celebration from the crowd, many waving triumphant betting slips in the air.

In the winner's enclosure the owner was called for, and a man in a top hat and swirling cape stepped forward. He held the rein lightly and smiled at the happy crowd.

As the cheers died down, a small child in the stands shouted, "It's Mr Antonio!"

The caped man took an extravagant bow and to everyone's amazement, Black Magic did the same, stretching out a long front leg and bending to touch it with his nose.

Then Mr Antonio flung back his cloak and reached up, hands on the jockey's shoulders. He twisted quickly, took off the jockey's head and held it above his own, to screams of horror from the crowd.

The jockey's mouth kept moving, "Thank you," it said. "Thank you. This is the proudest day of my life."

Meanwhile the jockey's headless torso, still astride the horse, lifted its arms to acknowledge the applause on all sides.

A child ran forward, the one who identified Mr Antonio earlier. "It's not real, is it?" he said. "It's one you made, like in your Galleria of

Anatomically Accurate Articulated Automata. Isn't it? And the horse, too?"

Mr Antonio swiftly took the jockey's body beneath one arm and, with the severed head under the other, he leapt gracefully onto Black Magic himself. He nodded down at the child, which made his top hat fall into the boy's hands. Mr Antonio winked, pulled at the reins, and kicked Black Magic into action. Within seconds he was on the far side of the track, then gone forever.

Some thought Mr Antonio a cheat, others a genius. Some thought they should have collected the odds from Black Magic's win, rather than have their betting stake repaid. Some thought the spectacle of not one, but two, perfectly formed automata was worth the confusion of the race.

And me? I think it was the most magnificent sight I've ever witnessed. And I still have Mr Antonio's hat.

My Hair by Chrissy Sturt

When little, my troublesome frizz was groomed away by an older sister who enjoyed smoothing me into something slightly less ugly, and wrapping me in ribbons.

Then, overnight, she was gone to live a grown-up life.

Who would tackle the terrible hair?

Mother's answer was a military crew cut; mistaken for an unfortunate-looking boy, I vanished into the family's slipstream.

And here I hid until teenage years when an experimental friend, all exposed midriff, push-up bras and magazine-fuelled ideas, plotted a drastic make-over. She secretly doused me in chemicals that stung and choked, and trapped us in a stink bomb of bleach and back-fired rebellion.

I was Casper-the-ghost level white.

Eventually I had to show myself.

Mother clutched her throat, flapped her hands – demanded the hairdresser *do something* – only expensive dye reacted with cheap dye, writhing across my scalp in a display of irredeemable orange streaks.

I became a warning against wildness, invoked by teachers when the class grew restive.

Nobody wanted to look like … *me*.

Hostile eyes flicked in my direction, before turning away.

I could relate; I didn't want to look like me either.

Until university, where budgetary constraints forced my hair to grow. It grew and grew, outlandishly and outrageously, forcing out of my scalp like playdough worms, until it was impossible to hide in any sort of slipstream, even if I'd tried. I was the river now, in full frothy spate, unstoppable; in possession of a lover who flipped me upside down and scrunched fistfuls of frizz into burning black spokes. *See, stunning*. Mysterious products were pressed into my unpractised hands. *You just need a little help*.

I looked squarely in the mirror; something nearing beauty skittered at the edges, like an artist's pencil drawn to potential. Perhaps I could be this version of me, after all?

I grew accustomed to the work required to produce these buttery curls.

They secured me a career and a husband, but motherhood rendered diffusing and defrizzing a time-hungry indulgence; I retreated to a sharp pixie cut, and tried to be something new again, another person, attuned to the needy creatures on my hip. I dropped kisses onto newborn heads, and hoped they wouldn't know the same agonies. Normal hair for my babies, please.

And what now, as I push on into middle age?

I am long, short.

Brown, blonde.

Black, red.

Straight, curly.

Up, down.

Tight, loose.

Styles as shifting as my moods.

People look to my hair for clues. Who is she today? What version is she unleashing on the world? It could be anything from glamour girl to grotbag.

The only consistency – the impossibility of pinpointing the real me.

Maybe turning grey will settle it.

Rachel's Visit by Marjorie Clifford

Rachel experienced an echo in her head from the door of the spaceship as she stepped onto the flaky ground. Hardly believing she had arrived at last. Travelling for several light years to this green planet named ZOG. All the visual tests and samples had already been taken. But could people colonize Zog? It was all trial and error. The satellite had performed tasks to prove that there was a possibility for life, it was her big chance to prove it, she had to try.

She stepped into the space walker repeating in her head what the scientists had said "We just need you to confirm if life actually exists on Zog."

The air was fresh in per space suit, and her chest still tight from breathing in a glass dome. Her legs cramped in her flight seat whilst entering the planet's gravity. All through the flight she was able to float about, it would be good to stretch her legs. The ground seemed firm enough, but the space walker was her safest bet. She could see a path lined with what Rachel thought were sunflowers.

She was taken to a circular building appearing from nowhere. It was turfed with blue grass that had merged with its surroundings. A rushing sound accompanied by a door opening and a riot of colours. A pleasant voice greeted her, but the being was not visible.
"RACHEL, WHY ARE YOU HERE?"
"You know my name, then you know why I am here?"
"WE ARE NOT SURE, WHAT IS THE PURPOSE OF YOUR VISIT?"
"I am visiting to see if this would be a safe place to live"
"WHO SENT YOU?"
"The scientists from Earth."
"THEREFORE, YOU WOULD WANT TO SEND OTHERS"
"Yes please, we are suffering from pollution and global warming on planet Earth, and we need help."
"THAT COULD BE A LENGTHY PROCESS RACHEL. THOSE WHO CAME HERE WOULD HAVE TO BE QUARANTINED FOR SEVERAL MONTHS."

"We wouldn't mind, if you would accept us to live on your beautiful planet."

"WHAT SKILLS WOULD YOU BRING? YOU HAVER TO PROVE YOUR WORTH"

"I have a degree in computing"

"WELCOME TO ZOG"

Rachel was then surrounded by beings all dressed in blue suits, wearing face coverings.

One of them spoke.

"Good morning, Rachel, welcome back. You have been asleep, under sedation for three weeks.

"We are going to see if you can breathe on your own by taking you off the ventilator. Please raise your hand if you would like to try."

Rachel raised her hand thinking.

"Well, she sounds down to Earth."

The Doctor said, "Nice and easy does it."

She was turned on her stomach and the air rushed into her lungs, breathing for herself.

Rachel had landed back in the real world. This after all was really living!

The House That Saved a Life by Lindsay Bertram

The old house stood alone on the empty block. Abandoned houses were standing as if the joy they once had, had been removed and left a lifeless building. For years it was alone, with little creatures living inside for company. The house had stood there for so long that he could barely remember when people had lived there. He especially liked children, with their pig-tails and G.I. Joe dolls. Every day he watched people walk by ignoring his creaking hello that he sang with his broken-down boards. He saw a young couple walking by. Even though he knew they would ignore it, he still sang his creaking hello. To his surprise, they went inside! He could see them walking up the stairs and onto the balcony. The most beautiful sunset on the horizon was the best thing they had ever seen. Just then, the old house heard the magic words, "I.LOVE.IT!" They bought him, and he was theirs. But he didn't know their names. One day the house heard the man calling for his wife. "Becky?". Her name was Becky and the man's name was...

"Yes, Charles?" Mrs. Becky answered. "Oh, there you are!" Charles said. "You need to see this!

He held up a 30-06 Springfield Cartridge. "Look what I found embedded in the stairs!

"And?" Becky said confusedly.

"This house was here in World War II! My grandfather was a Captain in the war. Why don't we use today for looking for clues?"

"Deal!" Becky said with a smile. "Why don't we look behind everything...couches...in-between floorboards... everywhere!!"

They hunted for two hours until Becky decided to look in the stairs. She decided to start from the bottom. She was near the middle when she found a hinge in the step. She tried opening it, but it wouldn't budge. She got a crowbar and pried it loose, and there inside the step was a yellowed envelope. She carefully opened the envelope and read the letter. She hurriedly called Charles and read aloud.

"If you're reading this, the war is over. This house saved my life and the lives of my soldiers. We were stranded, my soldiers wounded, and we retreated to this house. For over six days we stayed in the house with barely enough food. After the sounds had quieted, I went to the window to see if we were clear to go outside. Just as I looked out, someone shot the window. I had barely moved out of the way when the bullet pierced the glass and hit the stairs. If the old house had a slightly bigger window, I would be dead. After a few days, we escaped and survived the war. I would not be married to my dear wife Amelia, with my beautiful daughter Julia, without the protection this house provided.

    With that I say farewell,

        -Captain John Charles William

    Charles looked at Becky in disbelief, "Becky...my mother's name is Julia."

The Nearly Mother and her Woolly Jumpers by Denise Telford

'The trouble with being a shepherd is that you'll turn your back to put the kettle on and at least one bloody lamb will drop dead.'

Lola her name badge said, the woman in the shop delivering the blow. I was new to lambs, more a mummy than a shepherd.

'Oh, I'm sure they'll be fine,' I replied, moving further down the aisle to stop her words sticking.

I scanned the shelves, nonchalantly feigning interest in metal instruments for sale to 'castrate your own sheep.'

Lola had magicked a ladder and was climbing up to reach the very top of the shelves. 'Was it ten bottles you wanted?' she asked. I cupped my hands over my eyebrows to look up at her as if there was sunshine beaming down, blinding me. But I was in the Agricultural Shop, with artificial strip lights, half of which weren't working.

'Yes,' I said, 'ten bottles for ten little lambs.'

'Well,' Lola said, 'if you've got ten then you'll end up with six. If you're lucky.'

I was dumbstruck. The initial thrill at the prospect of raising these babies was becoming tainted by the creeping dread of their mortality.

'And another thing,' Lola shouted as I joined the checkout queue, 'for Christ's sake don't give them names.' She followed this with a roar of laughter as if what she had said was remotely funny.

I counted the lambs every morning at their 6am feed. Then again at lunch time and again when I locked them all up at night. I dreamt of foxes, sculking with straight backs on low legs, dragging them away by their tender long necks. Often, by torchlight, I'd march across the field, a maternal drive stamping out the shadow monsters. The lambs would hear me coming; start to bleat and prance on their little hooves. Pavlov's dogs under the inky skies. I brought no milk or cuddles just a belly full of dread and breath caught in my ribcage until I had counted all ten. Repeatedly.

After two weeks they became Holli, Phil, Baby, Michael, Betty, Augustus, Rupert, Jimmy, Diane and Alan. They had profile pictures taken to form a gallery for my Instagram feed. I washed their faces and taught them to lift their chins for tickles.

April brought showers, light and warm, in which they danced and bucked and jumped and ran.

And then came the first day of May. I overslept. A banging silence woke me with a start. My alarm had stopped. On auto pilot I made the bottles that I knew they would never drink, to never make them grow. In the stable they lay in a puzzle of patterned wool. Heads buried in each other. Chests still. No tiny beating hearts.

'It was likely that their mothers' herd was unvaccinated,' the vet said, 'we'll never really know.'

Sadness enveloped me and as I felt beneath my jumper for a thicker skin, he touched my shoulder, 'even the most accomplished Mother doesn't make a shepherd.'

The Night Marie Flew by Dee Holmes

'I'm staying tonight, Aly I just don't think there will be a tomorrow for Aunt Marie'

'I'll stay too' I was glad to hear her say that, I didn't want to stay here on my own. The lights had been dimmed now; the night noises had begun. Frail cries of distress, mutterings and calls to a nurse for no other reason than comfort, to know they were not alone.

It was sad, that my sister and I were the closest Marie had to children, having had none of her own.

We sat for an hour, maybe two, it was difficult to keep track of time. Had we slept? I've no idea. Aunt Marie was restless, making small noises as if she was having a conversation with someone.

Meanwhile in another world high above our universe, Donald was preparing for Marie's arrival.

He set about getting the Tiger Moth ready and fit to fly, he would collect his dear Marie and take her where they would be together at last.

Dressed in his airman's outfit of leather fur lined jacket, helmet and goggles, his air to ground radio headset hung around his neck.

He was telling anyone who cared to listen

'I fell for Marie the moment I saw her dancing at The Ritz' I outranked the fellow she was dancing with' he chuckled 'I made my move, and the rest was history'

Marie was beautiful, funny and an amazing dancer.

'Oh, I knew the dress she wore was made from the silk of a few damaged parachutes, but I never saw another girl who could wear a parachute as well as Marie'

Satisfied that he had done everything to ensure a safe journey, he threw the propeller, climbed into the cockpit and began his long journey.

My sister and I kept our vigil at Marie's bedside. She had a picture of Donald close by. She was never far away from that photograph. She had told us all about Donald on many occasions. Very many occasions in fact. But now she was making quiet murmuring noises, as if she was holding a conversation with somebody.

'Oh Donald' Aly and I both jumped when we heard her say that quite plainly, and again when the sound of a small plane could be heard flying very low over the hospice grounds.

'Come on Marie old girl, I've come to take you with me'

'But Donald, you went down with your plane'

'Don't believe all that old rubbish Marie, come on I've got the old crate idling, outside, waiting for us'

To our astonishment she raised her hand and a radiance replaced the dreadful pain on her face. We called a nurse

'I'm so sorry, your Aunt has gone I'm afraid'

Is it possible to laugh and cry at the same time, that's what we did? We knew for sure that Aunt Marie had gone in style. She was flying tonight with her darling Donald at last.

The Wonder of Woolies by Fay Dickinson

His favourite biscuits were the oblong ones with vivid orange icing. That's how they'd met. She'd served him in the days when Woolworth sold loose biscuits and customers pointed to the ones they wanted.

She was pretty and dainty in her blue-belted dress. Now her body's lumpy, her legs varicosed.

Bill bought lots of biscuits, not just the orange ones. before he dared to ask her out. Later he gave her a special nickname that made her laugh.

Woolworth was their shop. They bought crockery for their first home, clothes for the children, even foot spray, from the back of the shop, for Bill's golfing shoes which ponged somewhat in summer. It was always fun when they went there together and browsed the shelves. She remembered Bill holding up a pretty little dress of lemon yellow that he thought would just suit their youngest daughter. As he'd pressed the frock against his chest she had laughed, "It'll never fit you. We'll have to go somewhere else." They'd giggled as a rather prim assistant had given them a strange look. Mind you the same assistant had been all smiles when they bought the dress and quite a few other purchases shortly afterwards.

The pick 'n' mix biscuit counter disappeared years ago and now the shop itself is closing. The day before it shuts forever she takes Bill and they wander around the echoing store. The shelves have emptied fast just like Bill's brain. Small balls of fluff and odd scraps of paper wisp, rather sadly she thinks, across the floor and shelves She looks at the few unsold items: dusty electrical plugs, stickers and a forlorn-looking gift bag with a picture of biscuits on the front. She buys the lonely gift bag as a last memento of "their shop". Bill's eyes are as vacant as the shelves.

Back home she hands Bill a child's plastic lid-topped beaker of juice. He looks up, smiles and says, "Lily, you are the wonder of Woollies." His nickname for her. Excitedly she kisses his forehead. He glares and exclaims, "Who are you? Don't kiss me. Lily wouldn't like it." She moves back to her own chair and tries to cry quietly.

What's In A Name by John Bunting

When I came to, the body beside me was beginning to smell. Her time-worn face was sunk, her mad eyes staring blankly. Her skin was a mottled and sickly green, her white hair matted with thick, blackened blood. I rolled over onto my hands and knees, trembling, trying not to touch her. My stomach retched at the foulness. My head screamed *panic, hide*, but I forced myself to look again. *Who is she? What's happened to her?* Then my head won and I ran from that place.

Darkness was falling, but it made no difference to the swelter. I crossed the road into the Woods. Branches slapped me down and undergrowth tripped. A million insects swarmed my head and bit. I was not wanted here. I forced myself to stumble on until, exhausted, I crumpled onto a fallen tree. The night closed in, fearful, as if knowing what I did not. My senses swirled. *Who? Christ, did I do that?* I put my hands to my face and hummed softly, remembering the familiar, gentle rhythms and rockings that calmed me. I dreamt my nightmares.

The sun was high when I woke. The heat beat remorselessly through the trees, yet a chill was in my bones. My mind was clearer now. I had to go back; find who she was and what had happened. This time, the trees urged me forward, glad to be rid. I stepped quietly through the open front door and stood listening. Upstairs, men were talking. The chill circled my heart. *They've found her!* As I reached the top of the stairs, I saw them. A policeman and another man, standing over the body, handkerchiefs to their faces.

"All this blood!" gasped the policeman. He knelt down and felt around the back of the woman's head. "There's jagged bits of bone sticking out. Jeez, her skull's been split wide open."

The other man spoke, shaken. "Do you think someone did this to her?"

"Quite possibly, look at the state the room is in."
Me?

The policeman wiped his hands on his handkerchief. "What made you suspicious?"

"I wasn't. Her door's been open for several days, everyone's has with this heatwave. I just knocked to see how she was coping. I never thought…"

"No." The policeman stood up. "What's her name?"

"It's Mary Priestley. Old Ma Priestley."

Of course, Mary Priestley! How could I... hang on... The chill clawed and squeezed at my throat as I felt around the back of my head. My hair was dried and matted, and jagged bits of bone stuck out where my skull had been split wide open.

While I Wait at the Bus Stop by Lorraine Collins

Check time - 9.31 a.m. I'm early. Can't slow my racing heart. I'm checking it on my health app; two beats to every second.

Check time - 9.33 a.m. She said to meet here, before the Number 7 bus arrives at 9.45. No delays according to my timetable app. Twelve more minutes. I'll wait an extra ten after that then I'll go. That seems fair.

Check time - 9.35 a.m. Is this her? The woman crossing the road towards the bus-stop? No, she's too young, got EarPods in, talking into the air, waving her hands, oblivious to the traffic, not looking this way. I can hear her happy life floating towards me.

Check time - 9.37 a.m. Hang on, is this it, the bus I can see at the top of the road? Can't read the number from here. But it's a single decker, that can't be right. And she's not here. Why isn't anyone else waiting? Perhaps the bus isn't running today.

Check time - 9.40 a.m. She's still not here. Maybe she's changed her mind. I'll scroll the email again, make sure I've got the right bus stop. Think I'll hold my phone in case she's trying to contact me. Make sure it's not on silent. Put the ringer up to maximum.

Check time - 9.43 a.m. Maybe she's had an accident...I heard a siren earlier. Where's the nearest hospital?

Check time - 9.44 a.m. I hear footsteps to my right. I turn my head and see the shape of a woman, her image distorted through the prism of the graffitied Perspex shelter. This must be her, but she is not the image of my dreams. This woman is smaller, frailer, crumpled. Nothing special, insignificant. So just like me then. A spark of recognition ignites.

Check time - 9.45 a.m. The woman emerges and sits apart from me on the narrow plastic seat, ashen and panting. I look down at her ankles, mottled and swollen. It's safer than looking up. The bus pulls up. It's crowded. Is there room for two more? But she waves the bus away. The driver looks disgruntled.

We both check time - 9.47 a.m. She, looking at her wristwatch, little hands, big hands, faded strap. I, staring at my mobile, unfocused, but easier than looking directly at her. Keeping twenty-five years of distance between us.

"It's time," she says. Her voice is shaky. Now she turns and looks at me. Leans in. Drinks me in with red veined eyes, places a small blue veined hand over mine. She's all veins. We share the same blood pumping through them. She has faded needle marks on her arm and livid bruises flowering beneath her skin.

"When you were a baby, we got on the Number 7 bus and...I left you there. I'm so sorry...I just couldn't.... but now *I'm running out of time*...I wanted to stay with you while it passed by."

I look back at her. "Well," I say. "I've spent a lifetime waiting."

Black Matilda by Patrick Larismont

I've been here a long time. Long enough for a mighty oak to thrust fingerling roots through my yellowed bones and to see them thicken to the size of my thighs in life. The villagers wouldn't have me buried in the Lord Bishop's churchyard, saying I was a witch, but I never done nothing wrong. I didn't even know I was sick.

'Twas the year of our Lord 1348 when father brought me from our home county of Surrey to the harvest fair at the Farnham Hundred, on the lands of the Bishop of Winchester. I just a maid, past my fifteen seasons, and pretty, I'd been told but never kissed by a man that weren't my kin. I was there to help sell the woollens we'd toiled on all summer long. The great gathering was larger than anything I'd ever seen, and in my girlish curiosity I wandered the track, visiting the travellers making their way to market. Chattering Jews and brooding Scotsmen, red-faced Irish folk and all manner of foreigners bringing linens from France and lace from Flanders.

We'd paid our tithe to the Reeve, William Waryn, who looked an aged and feeble old man with a mass of white hair growing from his ears. He told us where to pitch our barrow and where water could be found for cooking and toiletries. My father sent me to fetch a pail, while he brushed down our mule and unloaded.

That eve there was merrymaking, but I was sent early to bed by father and was excited about what the morn might bring. I had a headache to my temple and my armpits felt tender, but thought it was the red ale I'd tried for the first time and that my monthly was due. By morning, I had a fever, was expelling green bile and had raised lumps on my skin. I died within three days and my poor blessed father just two thereafter.

The plague, for it was the Black Death, spread through the bishop's monastery and Farnham town, killing thirteen hundred Christian souls. Scared and angry, the survivors blamed my poor corpse, naming me Black Matilda and casting me to a pit outside the castle walls.

I've lain here ever since, the cold un-consecrated ground damning my soul for something I never done. I've watched this town ebb and flow and seen wonderous changes. Castles and monasteries have crumbled, replaced by wonderous roads and great cathedrals to commerce. Scholars, merchants, soldiers and clergy have all flocked here under the eyes of Black Matilda.

I've always been afeared though, this day would come, when a new malady stalks the town. I see it on the townsfolk's faces, blue masks to hold back the coughing contagion. It won't be long I fear before I'm joined by Covid Mary.

A third of the population of the ten villages in the Farnham Hundred perished from the bubonic plague in 1348. It was feared the village would never recover.

Farnham is Full by Anne Banks

"John……. John…. John!"

"Yes Mary! Stop shouting, I was just in the garage. What is it?"

"They're here! They're moving in." John stared up at his wife from the bottom of the stairs. She was pointing furiously out of the window on the landing. Her index finger jabbing the air repeatedly in the direction of No 34. "I can see a removal van. Good Lord. TWO removal vans. How much furniture do they have?"

"Mary, get away from the window they might see you."

"Don't be ridiculous, I'm entitled to look out of my own window. Anyway, I have this in case I'm spotted." Mary pulled out a bottle of Windolene Spray from her apron pocket and some scraps of kitchen towel. She smiled, thoroughly pleased with herself.

John stifled a laugh. "You really have thought this through dearest."

A few weeks ago, she had even called the Estate Agents who had dealt with the sale – determined to pump them for information. Alas, data protection had protected them from her more probing questions. The most they would tell her was that a sale had indeed taken place and that they would be delighted to come out and value their own house anytime that was convenient. Apparently, they had a waiting list of simply lovely families desperate to move to the area who were bound to pay a premium for their home. Mary had cut this conversation short. "Can you believe it? Yet another estate agent pushing us to sell. All these new families. Lord above. Farnham is Full! It is Full!"

And so today, Mary watched with bated breath as the new family moved in. Fresh from London. A toddler, a baby and a stupidly large family car. And then it came, the planning application. "John, it's scandalous! They've positively destroyed the garden. The roses and camelia are gone. I mean the wisteria!! How could they have pulled it out? It's ground zero over there. And now this."

John quite liked the look of the extension although he wasn't looking forward to the noise and building mayhem. "At least they haven't applied to divide the plot into two or to build flats on there dear." Mary, however, was losing sleep over No 34. It was all she could think about. Consumed by the change. Unable to prevent it. Her rage building until one day John heard a loud thud coming from the landing. He rushed up to find Mary unconscious on the floor. She'd fainted and was slowly coming back round. "Look…. Out…. There…. John…. Look." She pointed weakly towards the window. John looked out and saw large white van in No 34's driveway. The brand name proudly emblazoned across the side 'Astounding Astro Turf'. Large rolls of plastic lawn were being offloaded from the rear of the van. "Mary dearest, I think it might be time to get that valuation."

Missing by Dr Sarah Law

Audrey taped the last flyer to a lamppost in the Lion and Lamb Yard as the sun was setting, wondering how long before it was removed. She had spread them along the length of Castle Street, and all the connecting alleys and roads. She hadn't spied anybody taking them, nor following her. And yet for each 'missing dog' poster she placed, the one before had disappeared.

She sat on the edge of the black statue, the cobbled yards namesakes, swishing the optimistically carried leash, listening to the bustle of human traffic heading home.

Then the bustle stopped. She looked around; courtyard deserted. The street lamp shone in the twilight, but lights from shop windows were muted, as though seen from much further away, or through much thicker glass. A single distant dog bark broke the silence.

"Herbert?" She whispered. She hurried towards the high street. No people, no cars. Shop doors closed with drawn blinds and, when she looked closer, no seams in the walls. No hinges. No ledges or texture. They could be made out of paper, except for the fact she had always known them to be real.

A wisp of blue light caught her attention. She didn't feel afraid, perhaps strangely, but the wisp was far from her. She followed where it shone and then it darted ahead, appearing even further away, passing just around a corner. Again she heard the distant bark.

She reached the meadows, where the blades of grass didn't yield beneath her feet, yet the ground still felt soft. She crouched, testing with her hand. A huffing sound brought her head up, and there perched Herbert. Herbert made of silvery blue light, tail wagging, crouched in play. She laughed out loud and he dashed to her, licking her face, feeling more solid than the ground they played on.

She threw the ball in her hand and Herbert chased after it. Again, and again, until she tired of the game and they set off to wander, reunited friends.

They walked alongside the river under a bright moon, crossed the footbridge, pausing to play poohsticks. For Herbert this meant dashing off the bridge and down the bank, into the water and out again triumphantly as he shook his coat. She raised her arms to shield against the spray of droplets which failed to touch her.

As she lowered them, she blinked in the dawn. The cresting sun illuminated the top of the Blind Bishop's Steps, where she stood alone, flyers in hand. Leash dangling by her side. A cyclist from another time braked down the hill, not seeing or else not acknowledging her raised hand. She taped a flyer to the rickety fence. Just before the curve, where the verge lessened and the walkway came closer to the road, she taped another, next to a bunch of white flowers zip-tied to a post, above a photo of a girl long since ruined by rain. She looked back, and saw the previous poster had gone.

The Anniversary by Richard Fuller

You sit in the Victoria Garden in Farnham thinking about anniversaries. Your mother died fifty years ago this year, the saddest sort of golden jubilee. You never knew her, not really. You were only five at the time. No-one in your family ever speaks about it. So, you had to find out for yourself.

You look around. The sun is shining, and the flower beds are a glorious pallet of colour. There are roses, you recognise those, but not much else. Your mother it seemed, liked flowers, but no one told you. She would have approved of this place, known what each of the many-hued petals were.

Low box hedges, paths and benches mark out this small parcel of peace in the midst of the town bustle. A place where bees work tirelessly and caterpillars become butterflies. You think about why you are in this oasis of tranquillity, what brought you here. The not knowing what happened niggled, like a splinter under the skin. You had to dig till it came out. A robin hops on the flower arch, chirping. Other birds flit around.

It has taken a long time, many visits to libraries and hours on Google to get past the silence. But now you have your answers. You learned things you should have been told. Events that should have been divulged. You are sad that you had to find out the way you did. But at least now you know.

The answers brought you here, to this little known place. This place with its history of anniversaries. You look around at the small walled garden, with its mellow red-roofed shelter and sunken beds. Hard to believe this was once a swimming pool. Hard to believe it was built to commemorate the Diamond jubilee of Queen Victoria, and opened by daughter. Hard to believe that you find yourself here in this, Queen Elizabeth's, Platinum jubilee year.

You study it more closely and see that the sunken beds must have been the pool area, the shelter the changing room, and the raised margins the edge of the pool. You try and visualise what it must have been like when it was new. Men in their stripey swimsuits, women in long sleeved skirted costumes, barely an ankle and wrist on display. How different it must have seemed to the Lycra of today.

You learned that is it the ruby anniversary of the swimwear vanishing, of the pool closing for good. How sad it must have looked as it lay derelict until, like a butterfly, it emerged from its long cocoon of neglect and transformed into this beautiful garden, still with its royal connections, the Duchess of Gloucester performing the re-opening ceremony.

But all this is a digression. A distraction from the reason you found it and the reason you are here. You are here to see, in this tarnished golden jubilee year, the place where your mother drowned trying to teach you to swim.

The East Street Lamp's monologue by David Rowlandson

My first memory was like a religious experience. I was converted from gas to electric by order of 'his most high', the Farnham Architect supremo. I was fed the elixir of life. Electricity.

What I remember is, standing in East Street, surrounded by a cheering crowd. It had just turned dusk when suddenly I felt a jolt. Imagine my surprise when abruptly I was creating light and shadows in my vicinity. My head was like a beacon, shining into the corners of all the closest buildings and doorways. I wonder if I was the first electric lamppost in Farnham!

Farnham has always been associated with the army and I must admit I enjoyed their revelry on nights out at the Army and Navy pub, but that's been long gone. I have seen so many changes and enjoyed so much. The building of a theatre, named after someone called Redgrave I once overheard. Some nights I swear I swayed to the orchestral music escaping from the building.

In the last twenty years it's been the kids I have seen more often around here. Of all the years I have stood here, I have never seen so strange attire as those emanating from the Art school, or whatever it is called nowadays. Now and again, they painted me bright colours. Not sure that it pleased 'his most high', the Farnham Architect supremo. He always ended up sending out one of his underlings to tidy me up. I didn't mind. It was company and I always looked my best afterwards.

I have a friend; I'll have you know. A best friend. He comes around regularly to clean or change my bulb. He talks to me, but doesn't hear me when I respond. Humans! So unsensitive.

Everything's changing though nowadays. The cinema has gone, so has the theatre. I've watched as the shops and offices gradually crumbled under monstrous mechanical beasts. The dust and debris have so often settled on me, dulling my illumination capability. Worst of all, 'his most high', the Farnham Architect supremo, has forgotten me and I am no longer my dapper self.

Behind me are smart new buildings. I look so old fashioned and out of place. I don't see so many people passing me anymore, unless you count those working on building the tall metropolis that surround me, but they ignore me.

At night it has become lonely, only this odd old man with a bottle comes near me. He talks to me of his memories of Farnham and I wish I could tell him mine.

Oh! Oh! Here comes one of those mechanical carnivores. I guess this is where my light goes out for good. If they could have waited one more week, I would have reached my one hundredth birthday. Time stops for no-one. I believe they call this progress.

Printed in Great Britain
by Amazon